E        Robinson, Tom      c.1

Buttons

| DATE | | | |
|---|---|---|---|
| SE 19 '75 | MAR 20 '81 | MAY 8 '90 | |
| JUN 2 5 '76 | JUN '82 | | |
| OCT 28 '77 | NOV 28 '83 | MAY -5 '94 | |
| MAR 3 '78 | SEP 30 '83 | | |
| MAY 1 9 '78 | FEB 6 '84 | | |
| DEC 1 '78 | MAR 8 '85 | FEB 3 '95 | |
| | JUL 2 '85 | OCT 1 2 '97 | |
| FEB 2 '79 | | JAN 0 3 '11 | |
| MAR 23 '79 | MAR 1 '87 | | |
| NOV 30 '79 | Mar 25 | | |
| | FEB 15 '88 | | |
| DEC 19 '80 | MAR 3 0 '88 | | |

SUBJECT TO LATE FINE

© THE BAKER & TAYLOR CO.

# BUTTONS

# BUTTONS

BY TOM ROBINSON

DRAWINGS BY PEGGY BACON

NEW YORK · THE VIKING PRESS

Viking Seafarer edition
Issued in 1968 by The Viking Press, Inc.
625 Madison Avenue, New York, N.Y. 10022
Distributed in Canada by
The Macmillan Company of Canada Limited
Library of Congress catalog card number: 38–13327

Printed in U.S.A.
SBN 670–05011–3
3    4    5    6         74    73    72

E
C.1

# TO MARY BURKE

# BUTTONS

He was a cat.

He was born in an alley.

It was a back alley,

Very far back,

Back of all the rest of the alleys.

It was full of broken boxes and tin cans and old shoes and
other old things.

He was born in the back part of the back alley,

In an ash can

Almost full of ashes.

When he was six weeks old he opened his eyes one morning

And found that he was all alone.

He was very hungry.

He couldn't walk very well but he could roll like anything.

He rolled out of the ash can.

He ate anything that he could chew

Whether it was good for him or not.

It made him strong.

At first he climbed back into the ash can to spend the nights

Because the ash can was home.

When he grew bigger and stronger

He looked at his home and didn't care much about it,

So he started up the alley.

He was working toward the daylight at the end of it.

In these days he spent the night where he was when it

came.

Sometimes he met other cats.

At first these cats looked at him and let him alone

Because he didn't have anything they wanted.

When he got farther up the alley, he began to find things

that other cats wanted.

They tried to take them away from him.

Sometimes they did.

Sometimes they didn't.

When he got bigger and stronger

Nobody took anything away from him.

But they tried;

You could tell that by looking at him.

His ears were torn,

His face was scratched,

His tail was broken,

His fur coat looked ragged and moth eaten,

His legs were bent and twisted till he walked pigeon-toed

and bow-legged.

When all the other cats were afraid of him

He sat every night on the top of something and called them

names.

He wasn't dressed like a king,

But he was King of the Alley.

One day a new cat came into the alley.

He didn't know the king by looking at him

So he began to fight with him.

He was a good-looking cat to start with,

And well dressed.

But soon his clothes were badly torn.

He got scared and ran away.

Our hero ran after him.

He chased the strange cat from street to street.

They came to a tall tree.

Both cats ran up the tree

One after the other.

The strange cat jumped onto a near-by roof.

But he broke the top of the tree

And our hero was left in the lurch.

He was afraid to come down.

The fire department came and began to put a ladder up the

tree.

When he saw that ladder coming up,

He jumped into the house near the tree.

He jumped right through the glass.

He ran from floor to floor and room to room

All over the house.

He was looking for a way out,

But all the doors and windows were shut.

At last he ran down into the basement

And climbed into an ash can

Almost full of ashes

And went to sleep.

He was very tired.


When he woke up

He was not alone.

A man and a little girl were looking at him.

A plate of nice fresh kidneys was there beside him.

He ate the kidneys,

Then he washed up.

He hadn't washed for a long time.

He kept an eye on the little girl.

She said to the man:

"His fur is all in pieces.

"He ought to have buttons to hold the pieces together."

So they called him Buttons.


Buttons tried to get away, but he couldn't.

After a while he didn't want to.

He stopped scratching and began to purr.

His ears grew out.

His tail grew straight and his legs grew straight.

His fur coat got all soft and smooth.

He forgot he was an alley cat.

He began to look like a gentleman

And act like a gentleman.

By and by he was a gentleman,

And lived happily ever after.

He was a cat.

He was born in an alley.

It was a back alley,

Very far back,

Back of all the rest of the alleys.

It was full of broken boxes and tin cans and old

shoes and other old things.

He was born in the back part of the back alley,

In an ash can

Almost full of ashes.

When he was six weeks old he opened his eyes
one morning
And found that he was all alone.
He was very hungry.

He couldn't walk very well but he could roll like
anything.
He rolled out of the ash can.

He ate anything that he could chew

Whether it was good for him or not.

It made him strong.

At first he climbed back into the ash can to spend

the nights

Because the ash can was home.

When he grew bigger and stronger

He looked at his home and didn't care much

about it,

So he started up the alley.

He was working

toward the daylight

at the end of it.

In these days he spent the night

where he was when it came.

Sometimes he met other cats.

At first these cats looked at him and let him alone

Because he didn't have anything they wanted.

When he got farther up the alley, he began to
find things that other cats wanted.
They tried to take them away from him.

Sometimes they did.

Sometimes they didn't.

When he got bigger and stronger

Nobody took anything away from him.

But they tried;

You could tell that by looking at him.

His ears were torn,

His face was scratched,

His tail was broken,

His fur coat looked ragged and moth eaten,

His legs were bent and twisted till he walked

pigeon-toed and bow-legged.

When all the other cats were afraid of him
He sat every night on the top of something and
called them names.

He wasn't dressed like a king,
But he was King of the Alley.

One day a new cat came into the alley.

He didn't know the king by looking at him

So he began to fight with him.

He was a good-looking cat to start with,

And well dressed.

But soon his clothes were badly torn.

He got scared and ran away.

Our hero ran after him.

He chased the strange cat from street to street.

They came to a tall tree.

Both cats ran up the tree

One after the other.

The strange cat jumped onto a near-by roof.

But he broke the top of the tree

And our hero was left in the lurch.

He was afraid to come down.

The fire department came and began to put a
ladder up the tree.

When he saw that ladder coming up,
He jumped into the house near the tree.

He jumped right through the glass.

He ran from floor to floor and room to room
All over the house.

He was looking for a way out,

But all the doors and windows were shut.

At last he ran down into the basement

And climbed into an ash can

Almost full of ashes

And went to sleep.

He was very tired.

When he woke up
He was not alone.

A man and a little girl were looking at him.

A plate of nice fresh kidneys was there beside him.

He ate the kidneys,

Then he washed up.

He hadn't washed for a long time.

He kept an eye on the little girl.

She said to the man:

"His fur is all in pieces.

"He ought to have buttons to hold the pieces

together."

So they called him Buttons.

Buttons tried to get away, but he couldn't.

After a while he didn't want to.

He stopped scratching and began to purr.

His ears grew out.

His tail grew straight and his legs grew straight.

His fur coat got all soft and smooth.

He forgot he was an alley cat.

He began to look like a gentleman
And act like a gentleman.

By and by he was a gentleman,

And lived happily ever after.

3576